Summer Night Screams: Unexplainable Horror Stories

Summer Screams, Volume 1

Martha Wickham

Published by Martha Wickham, 2025.

This is a work of fiction. Similarities to real people, places, or events are entirely coincidental.

SUMMER NIGHT SCREAMS: UNEXPLAINABLE HORROR STORIES

First edition. June 1, 2025.

ISBN: 979-8231042906

Written by Martha Wickham.

Table of Contents

Knocking in the Dark

I'm a 27-year-old female from Flagstaff, Arizona. This happened about four years ago. At the time, I was living out of a converted school bus, traveling around the Pacific Northwest. You see all kinds of interesting ways people choose to live in buses or vans. I always tried to avoid the major metropolitan areas and preferred staying in smaller towns for overnight stops between destinations, but mostly, I loved finding secluded spots in national forests. Being deep in the woods with no one else around was where I felt most at ease, and I truly enjoyed the freedom of my nomadic lifestyle. I always felt it was inherently safer to be isolated in nature than to try to find inconspicuous parking in a busy urban environment. Sure, things could still feel a little spooky at night, but I always knew my odds were better when I was the only one out there. This particular week, I was slowly making my way between two larger cities in Oregon. I was taking my time, exploring the scenic byways and settling into remote campgrounds for several days at a stretch.

On this day, I turned off the main highway onto a narrow, overgrown logging road that disappeared into the dense woods. There were a few potential parking areas, but they all looked unused and as if no one had ventured down this road in quite some time, so I continued, hoping to find a more spacious and picturesque spot further in. Eventually, the road opened up into a wide clearing. It wasn't particularly scenic, just surrounded by a thick canopy of trees, but it was expansive, private, and quiet, and there was even a primitive rock fire pit in the center. I parked and leveled my bus. It was early summer, and it had been raining intermittently for days in Oregon, so there wasn't much to do outside. I opened the side door of my bus to let in some fresh air while I heated up some soup on my portable stove. It was nearing dusk, so I still had a few hours before I planned to go to sleep.

Over the next forty-five minutes, the last light faded from the sky, and the rain began to fall more steadily. I closed the door to keep the interior dry and instead slightly opened one of the small windows near the back of the bus. I sat on my makeshift bed and started watching a movie on my tablet, but about halfway through, a sudden reflection appeared on the screen from the open window behind me. It was a beam of light that vanished almost as quickly as it appeared. It didn't move away; it simply went out, as if someone had flicked a switch. When I turned around to look out the window, I saw nothing but darkness and the heavy rain. I had no way of knowing how far away the light had been or what had produced it.

Being on a road with other potential pull-offs, I tried to convince myself it was just another traveler, maybe their headlights briefly catching my window through the trees before they turned off their vehicle. However, the light hadn't seemed to originate from the direction of the main road I had come from. Behind my window were just trees. Perhaps there was another smaller track I was unaware of. There wasn't much I could investigate in the downpour, so I turned back around and continued watching my movie. Every now and then, I would glance out the windows or think I heard a faint sound outside, but with the rain drumming on the metal roof of the bus, it was impossible to distinguish real sounds from the weather. Each time I looked, though, I saw nothing to suggest anyone was out there, so I tried not to let it bother me too much. I'd guess it was around 1:00 AM when I decided to call it a night and try to get some sleep. I turned off all the lights in the bus, closed the remaining open window, and pulled down the blackout curtains. The interior was almost completely dark. I got under my blankets and tried to relax. Usually, I fell asleep quite easily, but tonight, sleep just wouldn't come. To make matters worse, the rain intensified, and after about an hour, distant rumbles of thunder started. It grew louder and closer, making it even harder to drift off. Around three hours into the night, above the sound of the torrential rain and booming thunder, I distinctly heard something move outside. It was just loud enough to cut through the storm. It sounded like someone or something running and snapping a twig on the ground somewhere very close to my bus.

As soon as I heard it, all other sounds seemed to fade away for a moment. It was so dark I couldn't even make out the ground directly beneath the window. The longer I stared into the darkness, the more uneasy I became. I had this strong feeling that someone else was out there, watching me. I quickly closed the window covering. I sat there, trying to rationalize it as my imagination playing tricks on me, but barely a minute later, I heard a voice. It was a low male voice, speaking in hushed tones, as if they were talking to someone else nearby. I remained completely still, too afraid to even lift the edge of the curtain to look out, knowing they would likely see any movement if they hadn't already. However, they probably already knew someone was inside the bus, which made the situation even more terrifying. There was a tense silence for what felt like a full five minutes, broken only by the relentless rain and thunder, before there was suddenly a sound right outside the side door of the bus. It sounded like something heavy scraping against the metal, as if someone was deliberately rubbing against the door. Then, there was a sharp rap.

A few seconds later, they rapped again, louder this time. Even though I was almost certain they knew I was inside, I was still too petrified to say anything. Maybe they weren't sure how many people were inside or if I was a man or a woman, so I felt safer remaining silent and still. A truly disturbing and anxiety-ridden ten minutes crawled by as the rapping continued every few seconds, without anyone saying another word. They had to be completely soaked by now and likely couldn't see much in this weather, but then, finally, they spoke again: "State Police, open the door!" There was no way I believed that. If it were actually law enforcement, wouldn't they have identified themselves clearly from the beginning? They persisted in rapping and calling out various phrases, all claiming they were officers and that I needed to open the door. This felt like a desperate tactic to get me to unlock the door without resorting to force. I cautiously edged the window covering aside and peered out.

All I could discern was a shadowy figure moving near the door, but based on their silhouette, they didn't appear to be wearing any kind of official uniform or gear. At that point, I was convinced this was about to escalate. I frantically weighed my options for what felt like a full minute as the rapping grew increasingly insistent before I decided my only chance was to risk getting into the driver's seat and trying to drive away. As soon as I moved to the front and started the engine, I heard two sets of running footsteps approaching the side of the bus. I started to pull forward just as a face appeared in the window right next to me. Thank goodness the bus didn't get stuck in the mud, and I managed to get back onto the logging road. As I drove away, I never saw any other vehicle on the road, which made the intentions of those unknown individuals seem incredibly sinister. I filed a report with the local sheriff's department, who, unsurprisingly, stated that no officers had been dispatched to that area that night, and I never received any further updates. Things could have turned out much worse out there, but thankfully, I haven't experienced anything like that since.

Summer Camp Nightmare

W

hen I was 11 years old, my aunt and uncle told me that they were sending me to a nature retreat for three weeks. I was a real homebody back then, and I guess sending me to this retreat was their way of encouraging me to develop social skills before I became too withdrawn or something. Looking back, I understand their intentions. No guardian wants to see their kid grow up isolated and unhappy. I suppose attending that retreat that summer did make me a bit more outgoing and better at interacting with people, but it certainly wasn't in the way they had imagined.

To say I wasn't thrilled about attending the nature retreat would be a massive understatement. When my aunt and uncle told me, I almost burst into tears right then and there. I promised that I'd do whatever it took to keep them from sending me to some wilderness ordeal for three weeks, that I'd try harder with my chores and be more helpful around the house. But they weren't looking to negotiate; they had made up their minds. I was going to the retreat whether or not I liked it, even if they had to practically carry me onto the waiting van. I'll be honest, I cried myself to sleep the night before departure day, and I was holding back tears during the drive to the meeting point where the van would pick us up. It was only when I was on the van with the other kids that I was certain I wouldn't cry anymore. And even then, I think it was only because I was frozen in apprehension at being surrounded by a bunch of boisterous pre-teens. A group of four kids actually asked what my problem was, and all I could do was just sit there, paralyzed with anxiety as they started speculating if I was unwell. It was completely mortifying, and I actually wondered if there was any way I could escape during a stop at a roadside diner or something. But then where would I go? What would I do? It was the very definition of being caught between a rock and a hard place, and obviously, I chose the hard place over the rock.

The first few days of the retreat were challenging, to say the least. I barely spoke to anyone, disliked the communal meals, and found the outdoor activities dreadful. I suppose I had been somewhat sheltered, having always eaten what I liked and slept in my own quiet room as an only child. So, the reality of eating somewhat bland food while sleeping in a shared dorm with five other kids was a significant shock to my system. My anxiety was quite high during that first week, but it was particularly intense during mealtimes, and that was entirely due to the fact that the boys' and girls' dorms shared a dining hall. It wasn't all the girls that made me so nervous either; it was one in particular, a girl named Olivia. She was the most beautiful girl I had ever seen: popular, kind, artistic, and self-assured. I spent almost all of lunch and dinner staring in her direction, except, of course, when her gaze turned my way. Then I would just focus intently on my plate, hoping she hadn't noticed me looking at her. I secretly wished she would come over to say hello while simultaneously hoping she would stay far away so I wouldn't become some stammering, red-faced idiot in front of her. Only one wish was granted, and it led to one of the most nerve-wracking moments of my young life.

I'll never forget how gentle her voice sounded from beside me, how she asked if the seat next to me was taken. I completely failed to give her a verbal answer, but she was confident enough to just smile softly and sit down, perhaps sensing that I was more thrilled by her presence than anything else in the world. I only managed to find my voice once she started asking me my name and where I was from and things like that. Hearing how interested she seemed in me and seeing the envious glances of some of the other boys in the dining hall was the first real confidence boost I had ever experienced. It didn't suddenly transform me into a social butterfly or anything; I was still somewhat shy and incredibly self-conscious, but for the rest of the day, it felt like I was walking on air. The same thing happened at dinner the following evening, with Olivia coming over to talk to me about various things. Only that time, I actually managed something resembling a complete conversation. And then, towards the end of my first week, when I had actually started to connect with two other fairly introverted and quirky guys, she finally asked me the pivotal question. Olivia walked up to the table I was sitting at with my two new friends and asked me if I wanted to meet her down by the old boathouse that evening before curfew.

Now, as you can imagine, something like that was strictly and utterly forbidden by the retreat rules. The boys and girls were not allowed to socialize outside of scheduled activities or the dining hall. But then, that's what made it so incredibly special to me. She obviously liked me enough to risk getting sent home early and in complete disgrace too. There had definitely been a time when an opportunity to get sent home early would have been something I would have eagerly seized. But after meeting and talking to Olivia, I didn't think I ever wanted to go back home at all. The risk made it exciting, even thrilling, and as nervous as I was about meeting her in private, I told her yes, of course, and then plotted how I would make my way down to the boathouse without being seen by any counselors. When the time came, my new friends wished me luck, offered some awkward advice on how to act cool, and then I set off towards the boathouse to meet Olivia.

When I arrived, my heart sank when I saw that she was nowhere to be seen. I was convinced that she wouldn't show, that I had gotten all my hopes up for nothing. But I was also terrified to just leave in case she showed up a little late and got the impression that I wasn't interested in her. I waited for five minutes, then ten. Then, when I eventually heard someone approaching along the path, who should emerge from the trees but the object of my affection, Olivia, and she was carrying two small blankets. As we talked, I was a mix of nervous and excited and apprehensive and joyful, but above all, it felt like some kind of victory. I could be sociable; I could potentially even have a connection with a pretty girl. Maybe I could even be more accepted if I put my mind to it, I thought. That might sound like my ego was inflating to dangerous levels, and you'd definitely be right about that. In fact, by the time Olivia had actually shown up, it had inflated to the point where I couldn't see how our little rendezvous could possibly go wrong. And when she suggested we take off our shoes and socks and dangle our feet in the water, I was so completely smitten that I didn't stop to think how that might not be the best of ideas.

We did take off our shoes and socks, then sat on the edge of the dock and put our feet in the water. The water was surprisingly warm, which in a way was a relief because then I couldn't pretend I was shaking from the cold and not because I was absolutely overwhelmed with nerves that such a lovely girl was spending time with me. We sat there for a while, talking quietly, and at some point, Olivia mentioned that she loved being near the water and that she often went kayaking on the lake near her home in Asheville. She told me that she could hold her breath for almost forty seconds, which was apparently quite good, and asked if I wanted to see her try. I would have happily watched her do just about anything at that point, so of course, I said yes. And when she slipped under the water, I counted up to thirty-eight seconds until she resurfaced, laughing. I was beyond impressed. Thirty-eight seconds is a long time. Then she asked how long I could hold my breath. I told her I didn't know, but I was more than willing to duck under so she could time me.

I remember ducking under the water and hearing her slightly muffled voice counting, loud in that sweet, melodic way she had. I counted along with her in my head, feeling my lungs start to ache for air as the seconds ticked by. But then, she suddenly stopped counting, and as I heard something splash into the water next to me, I instinctively kicked my legs to push myself back to the surface so I could see what it was. And that's when I felt a hand on the back of my neck, pushing me down and keeping me submerged as I tried to come up for air. I remember opening my eyes to see that Olivia was no longer in front of me, so whoever was holding me under was either behind me or had moved quickly. I began to panic, reaching up to pull the hand off my neck, but I couldn't. I had never been particularly strong, and the grip was firm. But then, since I was desperately low on oxygen, it was completely impossible for me to even budge. Within a couple more seconds, I could actually feel myself starting to black out. My lungs were burning, it got harder and harder to struggle against the force pushing me down, and there came a moment where I actually thought to myself, "I'm going to drown." The thought caused another surge of panic to run through me, but then after that, and this is the very last thing I clearly remember before I must have lost consciousness, was this strange feeling of peace and acceptance. I wasn't panicking anymore; I just sort of gave up trying to fight the feeling. Then, although I don't exactly remember it, I guess I just let myself drift off.

The next thing I remember was lying on the small beach, coughing up water while an adult voice was asking me if I could hear them. I was still disoriented, and in that moment, I couldn't fully recall what had happened. I was just confused and very tired. Then, as I looked around, I saw Olivia crying while one of the counselors tried to comfort her. It was only then that I actually remembered the hand holding me under the water. I had gone from the happiest I'd ever been to thinking I was going to die. I had no idea who had actually held me under, but Olivia did, and her guilt had her confessing to the counselor pretty quickly regarding who it was. Apparently, the whole thing had been a cruel prank orchestrated by a couple of other kids to mess with the shy, slightly awkward new kid. But she had no idea that they were going to try to literally drown me in the lake. From what I gathered, she panicked as soon as she saw them keep me under the water for so long and had rushed off to get a counselor so they could stop it.

The paramedics and the local sheriff arrived not long after. I was taken into the head counselor's office, and as you can imagine, it became a huge incident. What was intended to be just a stupid, mean prank had turned into what the sheriff's deputies were calling attempted assault. The kids involved were immediately expelled from the retreat that same night, and the one who had actually held me down ended up facing serious consequences. My aunt and uncle came to pick me up the next morning. My aunt gave the head counselor a stern talking-to before practically ushering me into the car. I hadn't cried when I went to the retreat, but I cried having to leave it. It was a whole mix of emotions too: happy to be leaving a place where I almost died, but sad to be leaving my first real friends behind, and sad to be leaving Olivia behind too. I know she was involved in the initial prank against me, and don't get me wrong, I definitely felt hurt and betrayed by that. But she also cared enough to run for help when she realized they were trying to actually harm me. I can't tell you how much that meant to me, and looking back, I do realize how strange that sounds. But in my naive 11-year-old mind, that was all the evidence I needed that she did actually care about me in some way, even if it wasn't the way I had hoped.

In a bizarre way, nearly drowning at that retreat turned out to be one of the most impactful things to ever happen to me. I realized that the worst thing in the world, death, wasn't actually as terrifying a concept when you came close to facing it. There comes a point of acceptance and peace. And after that, nothing really scared me anymore. I knew I could make friends; I knew I could be brave. And so, the things that I thought I could never do, like talk to people more easily or try new things, suddenly seemed possible. The only significant negative that came from it was my fear of deep water. I haven't gone swimming since that day, and the thought of being on a large boat honestly makes me anxious. Like I said, going to that retreat helped me overcome my social anxieties in a big way. It came at a cost, I suppose, but I still strangely am glad I endured the whole experience. Because now I'm not afraid of that one thing that grips so many other people and sometimes dictates their entire lives. I'm not afraid of death, and I guess that helps me live a little more fully than others.

Night Hike

I

n 2018, Alex drove to a national forest about six hours away. His goal was to hike up to an old ranger station that he was really eager to explore. He knew that entering or camping in it was technically prohibited because it was dilapidated and potentially structurally unsound. Alex had done some online research, and most accounts from around 2015 suggested it was relatively safe, but the most recent information he could find was from roughly five years prior, so he was quite uncertain about its current condition. He found a wide spot on the shoulder of the logging road where he could park. He then retrieved his pack with three days' worth of supplies and began the trek. For excursions like this, marked trails are usually nonexistent, so he relied on a handheld topographical GPS unit to ensure he was heading in the right direction, but in reality, he was mostly navigating through dense, uncharted woodland. The hike from the road was approximately six to seven hours. The deeper he ventured, the thicker and more uneven the terrain became. Alex was really hoping the ranger station would still be in reasonable condition for him to spend the night, but if not, he would simply have to locate another suitable spot nearby to pitch his tent and sleep.

After the rather exhausting six-plus hours of trekking through the forest, Alex finally arrived. He could see the structure appearing above the canopy, and as he drew nearer, it actually seemed to be in fairly good shape. The exterior siding was faded, naturally, but it looked structurally sound. He gave the porch railings a few firm shakes, and they felt quite stable, so he decided to try climbing the wooden steps. They were aged and groaned with each step, but seemed secure enough. Upon reaching the porch, Alex was momentarily struck by the panoramic views. He could see almost the entire valley. There were no signs of civilization – no buildings, roads, or houses – for what seemed like dozens of miles in every direction; just endless forest. After soaking in the vista, Alex walked across the porch and entered the station. It was quite small, unlike some of the larger ones that get renovated into vacation rentals or similar. This was just a single room, maybe 200 square feet. It contained a rusty cot in one corner and a weathered metal desk in the opposite corner, with cracked windows lining the entire front wall. There wasn't much else inside, so Alex set down his pack and unrolled his sleeping pad and bag, then heated up a dehydrated meal on his compact backpacking stove. As dusk settled, he stepped back out onto the porch and watched the sunset. It was easily one of the most breathtaking sunsets he had ever witnessed. It seemed to fade quickly, though, and then total darkness enveloped everything. The sky was clear, however, and a brilliant full moon illuminated the landscape, casting long, eerie shadows. With nothing else to do, Alex remained sitting on the porch for some time. It was probably around 1:00 AM when he noticed something below. There was a beam of light moving erratically among the trees. What was peculiar about it was that it didn't seem like a standard flashlight. It had a soft, yellowish glow and pulsed gently, almost like a lantern. The light was moving through the trees in the woods not too far from his location. The odds of encountering someone else out here at the same time as him in such a secluded part of the wilderness were extremely low, especially considering there wasn't even a marked trail to get here.

Furthermore, navigating at night without a conventional flashlight and using what appeared to be a lantern was rather unusual. Alex watched as the light weaved through the trees for about twenty minutes, then it disappeared behind some dense foliage, and he couldn't see it anymore. For the next hour, he didn't see it reappear. He continued to sit on the porch, enjoying the tranquility and silence of the night. Eventually, a light breeze began to make it a bit chilly, so Alex stood up to take one last look before going inside. However, when he glanced down from the porch, someone was standing there. They were in the clearing between the ranger station and the treeline, looking directly up at him. It might have been the person with the lantern he had seen earlier. "Is everything alright?" Alex called out. He wasn't sure what else to say. They didn't move or respond verbally. There was just this strange period of about fifteen to twenty seconds of them looking at each other before they slowly raised their hand in a sort of hesitant wave or acknowledgement, then they turned and walked silently back into the woods, still without any visible light. Naturally, this was incredibly unsettling and strange, but for some reason, in that moment, Alex felt almost certain that it was just another backpacker intending to stay in the station who was perhaps surprised to see someone already there. Maybe they were just looking up to see if the place was occupied. Why they hesitated to answer and only offered a wave, he couldn't say. Alex stayed outside for a little while longer, but seeing nothing else, he went inside and got into his sleeping bag to warm up. It was a bit difficult to fall asleep due to the wind rattling the loose windowpanes and the old wooden structure groaning occasionally, but eventually, he did drift off.

It's hard to say exactly how much time passed, but when Alex awoke, the breeze had died down, and it was still very dark outside. He opened his eyes, wondering what had caused him to wake up, and then he heard a distinct sound: the faint squeak of the wooden steps outside. Alex sat up, thinking he must be mistaken, but then he heard it again and again. Someone was climbing the steps. He couldn't tell how far up or down they were; he could just hear the dry creaking of the aged wood with each step they took. Outside the windows, however, it was pitch black. Alex unzipped his sleeping bag and stood up, his heart pounding as he grabbed his backpack and moved towards the doorway. During the fifteen or so seconds it took to reach the door, the creaking grew louder and faster, as if they were hurrying, before it abruptly stopped just as he reached the doorway. Alex stood frozen for a moment, listening intently for any other sound, then he cautiously stepped out onto the porch and peered around the corner towards the steps. No one was there. He carefully moved closer and felt his pulse quickening as he leaned over and looked down. The steps were empty. Alex was in a state of shock for a brief moment, confused and terrified and completely unsure of what was happening.

Then, a sudden series of rapid footsteps echoed from the far side of the porch behind him. He only caught a fleeting glimpse of a shadowy figure darting between the support pillars on the other side. Alex didn't hesitate; he quickly swung his leg over the porch railing and scrambled down the steps. It was a terrifying descent down the weathered wooden steps as his entire body trembled with adrenaline, with someone seemingly chasing him from above. He reached the bottom and plunged into the dense undergrowth. Honestly, he doesn't know why he even instinctively grabbed his backpack when he woke up to investigate the noise, but it turned out to be the best decision he could have made, possibly even saving him. With his headlamp and GPS in his pack, Alex was able to navigate his way out of there and back to his vehicle. As far as he could tell, he wasn't followed. He drove away and didn't look back.

Accidental Betrayal

C

ynthia, a woman of 45, carried a deep-seated distrust for a particular holiday. Her adoptive parents, Emily and David, had welcomed her into their lives when she was just two months old. Her birth parents, facing financial hardship at the time, had made the difficult decision to give her the opportunity for a better life. Emily and David had been, and continued to be, her unwavering support system. Cynthia was eternally grateful for their love and care, especially considering the events of that fateful night.

Halloween had once been a cherished time for Cynthia. She enjoyed spending it with friends and family, decorating her home, and delighting in the neighborhood children's playful frights. She particularly loved sipping on spiced cider while sharing spooky tales with her neighbor's two kids, whom she often babysat when she was home from her work in another state. One year, she was home for the long weekend and was making the most of her time with her parents before returning. Emily needed to make a last-minute trip to the market, and Cynthia decided to accompany her.

They had been walking down the street for about thirty minutes when Cynthia began to notice people casting strange glances their way. This continued for another few minutes before she leaned towards her mother. "What are they looking at?" Cynthia asked. "They're staring at you," Emily whispered. "Why, though? I don't know any of them," Cynthia frowned. "Don't think too much of it, honey. They probably just confuse me for someone else." "Probably," Cynthia murmured, but the unsettling looks lingered in her mind. They finished their errands, had lunch, and returned home to prepare for the evening.

The scene that awaited them at home was bizarre. David was watching the news and saw a picture of Cynthia. Apparently, she had robbed a convenience store and assaulted the clerk earlier that week. What baffled Cynthia the most was that she had never committed any illegal act in her entire life. The fact that she was wanted for a crime she didn't commit sent Emily into a state of high anxiety, muttering about the potential consequences. David seemed to understand her unspoken fears.

The police arrived at their house, arrested Cynthia, and took her in for questioning about the robbery and assault. They eventually released her but instructed her not to leave town, stating they would be in touch if they had further questions. Her family was outraged. The entire ordeal made Cynthia feel sick to her stomach. She retreated to her room for a while before being awakened by someone screaming downstairs. She rushed down the staircase to see a young woman who looked exactly like her yelling at her parents. She was demanding to know why they hadn't taken her too. It turned out that Cynthia had an identical twin sister. Her parents had adopted Cynthia after another family had adopted her sister. Cynthia had, by all accounts, received the better end of the adoption. Her parents were financially stable, educated, and had successful careers, whereas her twin's adoptive parents were involved in illegal activities, and her sister had endured a life of abuse. She had dropped out of school, never attended college, and worked as a performer at a club in a neighboring city. Her adoptive parents had told her about Cynthia when she was nineteen. It had taken her a few years to finally locate her, and she had been stalking Cynthia for months after finding her. This twin sister was committing crimes in Cynthia's town, and people were mistaking her for Cynthia, all because Cynthia had been unaware of her twin's existence. Her twin sister, under the influence of some kind of drug, was enraged and, finally losing her temper with Emily's pleas for her to leave them alone, shot Emily in the leg. The sister fled the house. Cynthia called for help, and Emily was rushed to the hospital. The police later apprehended Cynthia's sister for attempting to rob a pharmacy a few blocks from Cynthia's house. She was charged with the crimes she had committed and sentenced to twenty-five years in prison.

Her sister occasionally sent Cynthia letters, filled with threats against her and her parents, unable to let go of the bitterness that Cynthia had a better life. At times, Cynthia was still astounded by the fact that her twin even existed. It felt like something out of a terrifying movie. While she felt a sense of pity for her sister's difficult life, she knew it was not something she could have prevented. It had happened, and now, that particular holiday held no joy for Cynthia, all because of her estranged and troubled twin.

The Backwoods Eater

M

ark took his wife, Julia, and their three kids to his parents' farm out in the country. They had a vast property there that his kids loved to explore and a spacious house that Julia often mentioned wanting them to move into. The only complication during this particular trip was that Julia had invited her parents to stay with them for the weekend.

Mark loved Julia, but he found her mother incredibly irritating. It only took a few hours for her to frustrate him to the point where he couldn't bear to be around anyone. He couldn't sleep that night either, his mind replaying his mother-in-law's comments with escalating annoyance. Around 3:00 in the morning, Mark decided to go for an impromptu hunt. He didn't care about actually finding or shooting anything; he just desperately needed to avoid his in-laws for the day. He always kept his hunting gear at his parents' place in case the urge struck, so he loaded up, left a brief note for Julia, borrowed his dad's old lever-action rifle, and headed into the pre-dawn woods. He made his way to one of the tree stands he used to hunt from as a teenager, climbed up, and settled in. Soon after, a wave of sleepiness washed over him, so he decided to nap until daybreak. However, he was awakened shortly by the strangest noise he had ever encountered. He couldn't determine if it was an animal retching or someone laughing; it was just these awful, guttural cries. Mark stood up quietly and peered outside. Dawn was approaching, casting a faint glow of light, barely enough to make out shapes.

Through his scope, he spotted something a distance away, but he only caught a fleeting glimpse of it before it darted behind a large oak tree. He could hardly believe it, but it looked like a person. So, he sat there, his gaze fixed on the tree, waiting for something to reappear. He didn't want to shout in case it was actually an animal he wouldn't want to scare off. Eventually, full daylight arrived, and nothing had happened. Mark gave up, concluding that he had likely just imagined things in his groggy state, probably just a sick animal that had climbed into the tree. By then, he was getting hungry, so he carefully set up his small backpacking stove inside the blind. He knew it wasn't the safest practice, and the smell of food could deter deer, but he didn't care about anything but being alone. He had brought some granola bars, a thermos of his dad's homemade stew, and some instant coffee. He started heating water for the coffee while he munched on a granola bar. The quiet hum of the stove allowed him to still hear what was happening outside. The water wasn't even warm before he started to hear movement nearby, and it sounded fairly large. He grabbed the rifle and looked outside, but he couldn't see anything in that direction. He thought maybe he had moved too loudly, or the smell of the propane had scared it away. However, just a few seconds later, he heard the same noise again, even closer this time, but from the opposite direction. He looked over and again saw nothing. Frustrated, Mark lowered the rifle and stepped away from the wall, only to hear something from just outside the door. He looked through the small opening, and this time, there was definitely something out there, but it wasn't what he had hoped for.

Ten yards away, the face of an old woman was peeking out from behind a thick pine tree. She was smiling, her mouth devoid of teeth, just red, swollen gums. Her skin was a sickly yellow, and she had no hair on the top of her head, just a few thin, white strands. The sight of her shook Mark, causing him to stumble backward, spilling the hot water and granola bar crumbs all over the floor of the blind. He rushed to turn off the stove before it caused a fire, and in those brief seconds, the woman outside had closed the distance between them. Mark was still on the ground when she opened the door, standing over him. She looked even more gaunt up close, like a skeleton draped in nothing but a filthy, ripped nightgown. He scrambled and reached for the rifle, expecting her to attack, but she immediately dropped to the ground and started eating all the spilled granola bar crumbs without hands.

Trapped in the small space with her, Mark just crawled back into the corner, his rifle clutched in his hand, and watched her lap up every single piece and swallow it whole, like a starved animal. He couldn't comprehend what he was seeing – a human, an animal, something else? Would she turn to eat him when she was finished? Sure enough, when all the food on the floor was gone, the woman looked at him and started crawling towards him. She was staring into his soul with her mouth open, making those same horrible grunting, heaving sounds he had heard earlier. Panicking, Mark grabbed the thermos of stew sitting next to him, opened it, and quickly slid it over. The woman picked it up, sniffed it, then stuck her tongue out and licked across the entire surface, as if claiming it. In less than a minute, she had drunk the entire contents and licked the thermos clean. It was the most repulsive thing Mark had ever witnessed.

When he realized she was about to demand more food, and he had none left, he seized the last opportunity while she was distracted and bolted out of the blind. He took only the rifle, letting her rummage through the rest of his belongings, and ran all the way back to the farm. He would rather face his mother-in-law than discover the extent of the danger he had been in with that horrifying creature in the woods. He told his family about it and reported it to the local police, but everyone seemed to just dismiss it with a laugh. One boy did tell him his friends informed him there was a homeless hag that lives out there, and if you don't feed her she'll steal your soul. The officers did search the area around his parents' property, but they never found any trace of the woman. To this day, Mark still has nightmares about her. What if he hadn't brought food? Would he have been the next meal? Did that woman just live in the woods around his parents' farm? All he knew was he was never moving back there to find out.

A Camping Trip Gone Wrong

P

riya and her two close friends Rohan and Sam were eagerly anticipating the long weekend because they had planned a camping trip to the Whispering Woods National Park in Oregon. Priya was incredibly excited as this was her first time camping with the boys.

Finally, on Friday evening, they arrived at the campsite. They were all having a wonderful time, sharing spooky stories around the crackling fire. "I absolutely love grilling and camping! Oh my gosh, I had to practically beg you guys to come. Look how much fun you're having thanks to me! We thought you'd be too scared to camp at night. Seriously, I'm braver than both of you!" Priya let the guys know.

"We'll just see about that. Spend one night out here in the woods without running off, and we'll see who the real brave one is," Sam told Priya.

She stood up and looked him in the eyes. "You're on."

Around eleven o'clock, Priya began to feel a bit sleepy and went to her tent to rest.

After she left, Rohan and Sam also went to sleep in their tent. In the middle of the night, Priya was awakened by a strange howling sound. She became frightened and went to the boys' tent to ask if they had heard the odd noise. "Rohan, Sam, wake up! I heard this really weird howling sound in the woods. Did either of you hear anything?"

Sam told Priya that he hadn't heard a thing. "Didn't someone just claim they were brave?"

"Nothing scares you." Seeing Priya so terrified, Rohan started teasing her, which only made Priya more upset.

To cheer her up, the boys decided to go outside and check around the tent to make sure everything was okay. They reassured her, "Don't worry, we'll be right back."

Priya waited for the boys in their tent, but even after half an hour, they hadn't returned. Priya started to panic even more. She tried calling them several times, but the signal was too weak for the calls to go through. Eventually, Priya gathered her courage and decided to venture out into the woods to look for them. The forest was completely dark and chilly. Priya felt extremely terrified walking alone in the forest. A wind blew and in it seemed to be whispers she couldn't understand. She wondered how she would make it through the night and went back to the tent to put on her jacket. "Guys, come on out! Seriously, this isn't even funny anymore! Please! Oh my goodness!" She stepped in something thick and sticky. She made a face and when she turned the flashlight on from her phone she saw a dark red mess leading into the deep forest. She followed it and the blood trickled on until it stopped at a tree where there was another pool of blood. The four footprints stopped as well.

She ran down the blood trail, scooped up her small tent into a quick mess, threw it into her car and began driving down the dirt road. The whispering wind seemed to be following her!

Priya was driving as fast as she could to get out of there. "Oh, I wish we had never planned this camping trip! I wish I hadn't pressured the guys to come! This is all my fault." Those were her last words until she hit the highway and pulled over to call the cops.

Dark Escape

Two years prior, in October, Maya and her husband, Mark, took a trip to Sequoia National Park. They were staying just outside the park in Three Rivers. One evening, as they were driving back from the Giant Forest, Maya noticed their headlights illuminate what appeared to be someone lying down on the shoulder of the road, both feet pointing towards the street. Maya told Mark that there was a person lying in the pitch black on the side of the highway.

Mark, knowing Maya's interest in true crime, was absolutely certain that what she had seen was just discarded items. Maya, however, was adamant. "No, I saw a body. I know it was a person." They made their way back to their rented cabin, and as they were about to park, Mark looked over at Maya and said, "You're really sure about this, aren't you? You want to go back?"

Maya was resolute. "Yes." As they drove by again, Maya saw the feet she had noticed earlier. She had Mark turn the car around and yelled at him to stop.

He rolled down his window and called out, "Hey, are you okay?" There was no answer. He tried again, even louder, "Hey, are you okay?"

Suddenly, the woman, dressed entirely in navy blue, sat up. She was wearing a nice quilted jacket, dark pants, and had her handbag and two water bottles with her. Her makeup esas neatly done, and she seemed very polite. Mark was visibly taken aback. Maya asked her where she was headed. The woman said that she was trying to get to the gas station up the road and that her sister was going to meet her there to pick her up. This woman appeared to be in her early 50s. Maya sensed that something was amiss because where they had found her, the gas station was still another five miles or so away.

The woman said that in her mind, she thought it was only about half a mile from her motel and that she could walk it. They offered her a ride, and she climbed into the back seat, but not before Maya instinctively grabbed a thick shawl to wrap around her neck, her pepper spray discreetly within reach.

As they drove, they tried to engage her in casual conversation. Maya asked why she had been lying on the side of the road. The woman said she had gotten tired of walking and had simply decided to lie down, seemingly ready to give up. It was late autumn, and she had no hat or gloves on. Maya could tell she was very vulnerable.

Once they arrived at the well-lit gas station, the woman thanked them, got out of the car, and sat on a bench in front of the open convenience store. They offered to stay with her until her sister arrived, but she declined, saying she would be fine. Maya reminded her that cell reception could be spotty in the area and double-checked that she didn't want them to wait with her. They drove back to their cabin and noticed that there were now three sheriff's vehicles in the parking lot. They had not been there the first time they had arrived back from the park that evening. Maya told Mark that she knew they had to be there for that woman. She calmly walked over to one of the cars and asked if they were looking for a missing person, a woman. The deputy told her that they were and asked if she had seen her. Maya explained the situation and that she really felt like something very bad had happened to the woman. He thanked them for picking her up and giving her a ride. He couldn't disclose what had occurred but implied that her leaving and going somewhere else was a wise decision.

Maya asked that he go check on her at the gas station just to make sure she was okay and that her sister did eventually arrive. Maya was realizing that whatever had happened was likely at the same motel where they were staying that evening. She later looked up the local police blotter and found that a domestic disturbance call had come from their motel. The woman had been seriously assaulted and was so terrified that she was willing to walk in the dark without a flashlight just to escape. Maya guessed that after walking about a quarter of a mile from the motel, she was in so much pain that she had simply needed to lie down, perhaps feeling like she might actually die there.

She couldn't go back to the motel because she had already escaped and gone to the front desk to call her sister. Her attacker would have known she had been there and might have come after her. The front office had called the police for her while she fled. It was Maya's understanding that the man who had hurt her was her boyfriend and that he was arrested. Maya often wondered about the woman and whether she had gone back to him, if her sister had ever picked her up, and if she was safe now. Mark always listened when Maya said there was someone in need on the side of the road.

Haunted Double

T

his story comes from Maya, a childhood friend, who recounted this experience that still unnerves her to this day. She was genuinely freaked out, and her family corroborated her claims. Here it goes: Maya and her family moved into this rental property in the summer of 2019. Maya claimed that it was haunted. Everyone agreed that there was an unsettling atmosphere, and those who visited or stayed over would mention it as well. I myself experienced this odd feeling of foreboding whenever I went over there and believed the consensus that the house was indeed haunted. It honestly felt oppressive inside there, and you would feel this pitiful dread that is hard to put into words. It was extremely uncomfortable to experience, to say the least. Anyway, this particular event, which is the basis of this account, was enough for Maya's family to pack up and stay with relatives until they moved out permanently a few weeks later.

On this fateful afternoon in late July, Maya had arrived back home from the community pool and heard an argument taking place in the kitchen between her mom and dad. Maya thought this was strange as both of her parents should be at their respective workplaces, so she called out "Mom?" before unlocking the front door and going inside. Maya said the house fell instantly silent, an uncanny silence like all the air had been sucked out of the place. It felt stifling, felt wrong. Then her mom said, "Hey, um, we're just in here." Maya was just outside, closed the kitchen door at this point, and froze. It was her mother's voice beyond the closed door, but there was something off, like the usual cadence was missing that made it recognizably her mother's. It sounded flat and unnatural. Maya decided to bolt back out the front door and wait until her brother came home, but she said as she turned back, she saw her mother peering at her from the living room window. But it wasn't her mother. The face was the same, everything was the same, but her face was devoid of anything that actually made it her mother. There was no recognition on her mother's face, no indication that she was looking directly at her daughter, no emotion in the expression, nothing. The eyes looked unblinking. Maya screamed and ran down the street to her mother's workplace, a bakery a few blocks away, and confirmed that her mother was there the entire time and had never been at home.

Initially, Maya's mother reasoned that someone must have broken in, but a later investigation proved nothing had been stolen. The back door was locked, as was the front door when Maya came home. No one could rationalize who Maya saw in the window and why it looked so much like her mother, so that was the deciding factor to nope out of there and find somewhere else to live. The landlord of the house denied anything like this had happened while they lived there but did admit that the tenants didn't stay long, saying there was something "off" about the house. Maya also told me that she was the only one who actually saw anything definitively sinister inside that house, but her family said they definitely felt an evil presence there, which ultimately manifested into the doppelganger experience that Maya had had. Utterly terrifying.

Silent Evil

T

his story takes place about eight years ago, in early January of 2017. Jake was a senior in high school at the time, and it remains the single most perplexing thing he has ever experienced. It's also important to note that it happened in the middle of January. Jake is from North Dakota, and the winters there get brutally cold at night, the kind of cold where getting stranded outside could be fatal. That, combined with heavy snowfall, creates an eerie silence where you can hear everything inside the house and even just outside.

Jake and his best friend, Ryan, were hanging out in Jake's family's finished attic, just passing a boring winter night playing video games. They were also the only ones home. Jake's father had gone straight from work to a bowling league, so Jake and Ryan thought it would be a good idea to sneak a bottle of his father's expensive scotch and live a little.

As they were sitting there, carefully opening the seal on the bottle, Jake heard the door to the attached carport open and then slam shut. He immediately thought, "Oh crap," and started looking for places to hide the bottle. Ryan then said, "Hey, I thought your dad was supposed to be out all night?" "He was," Jake replied, then he heard a few heavy thuds and his father yell out, "Anyone home?" Jake yelled back up the stairs, "Yeah, just hanging out in the attic." He heard a few more steps moving from the carport door towards the attic stairs, and then his father yelled out again, "Hey, can you come down here? I need your help with something. I need you up here." Jake replied back while frantically trying to find a good place to stash the scotch bottle, "Yeah, just... just give me a minute, Dad." Then there was silence for about fifteen seconds. "Anyone up there with you?" his father yelled back in a more concerned, serious tone, in a voice that was slightly off from his father's usual tone. This was the first thing that made Jake feel uneasy. His family never cared if friends were over, as their house was always open to family and friends, and his father's voice just sounded wrong. It sounded like his father, but it was missing something that Jake couldn't quite pinpoint. "Weird," Jake replied back. "Just Ryan."

After he yelled that back, Jake found a decent hiding spot for the bottle and began walking down the steps to the next level. Now, as he was walking down the steps, he couldn't shake the overwhelming silence of the house and a slight electric tingle in the air. Something didn't feel right. When he reached the bottom of the short staircase, he looked over to where the door to the carport was, and also the laundry room right next to it. It was black, pitch black. All the lights were off, and there was no moonlight filtering through any windows. Jake walked over to the laundry room doorway, yelling out, "Dad, where are you?" No reply. The silence and darkness made the electric tingle intensify into full-blown prickles of fear. His adrenaline started pumping. He had to get out of there as fast as possible. His father was not home. Jake ran back up the short stairs, grabbing his jacket along the way. "What's wrong, Jake?" Ryan asked, looking confused. "My dad's not home," Jake replied quickly, looking for his car keys. "What do you mean? You were just talking with him." Jake could see the bewilderment on Ryan's face. "Look, man, there's no one home. We need to leave now." Jake took a few steps towards the back door that opened into the snowy yard. He saw his dog whimpering on the rug and his cat hissing from under the kitchen table. He couldn't leave them and just knew if they left them, something bad would happen. "Are we leaving?" Ryan said, still confused.

"No, I... I can't leave them here alone. Something is really off, though. I'm going to call my dad and figure this out." Jake pulled out his phone and called his father.

He picked up immediately. "What's going on?" he answered. "Dad, were you just home? I heard you yelling for me from the second floor, and when I went down there, you weren't there," Jake said, hoping that his father was playing some kind of joke.

"No, son, I'm... I'm just leaving the bowling alley. I wasn't feeling too great. Are you okay? What do you mean you heard me?" Jake filled him in on the whole story, and his father said he would rush home. Jake and Ryan stayed up in the attic with the animals until his father got there, but before he did, they could hear something downstairs.

Not walking or touching things, but a pressure in the air, like a void was slowly moving from one room to the next. The word that Jake would instinctively use to describe it was "hungry." When his father got home, you could feel the thing leave just as quickly as it had come, like an oppressive, predatory presence had just vanished. They have still never figured out what the hell was going on. This is just one story of many unexplainable things that have happened to them, but this is the easiest one to recount and the one that Jake was glad Ryan had witnessed. Jake's father has passed away now, and Jake has moved to Colorado, but whenever he goes back to North Dakota and sees Ryan, they still get creeped out by what happened. Jake will truly never know what took place that night, but he knows whatever it was that had his father's voice, it felt malevolent and hungry.

The Tech Ghost

T

he three camp counselors snuck around the cabins while the campers slept. The speakers for the fake ghost sound effects were hidden behind trees in bushes. They weren't easy to find and it was a clear night. They could hear owls, crickets, and frogs. The moon was almost full, but this prank would go on for a few nights. Just long enough for the campers to think there was a real ghost in the woods.

They placed the last fake haunted item on the table by the window. A smart phone with a ghost hunting app. It was left on so when an occasional fake ghost was detected, it would appear on the screen in red and scream loudly. They snuck through the door, turned the lock, and closed it slowly.

The counselors Tina, Brianna, and Terry ran to their bunks and turned the sound effects on. The chains rattling and ghostly moaning didn't wake the campers at first. Come midnight they started waking up and wondering what the chain sounds were. The ghostly moaning was what scared them. Suddenly the phone on the table screamed loudly. "What is that?" Johnny asked.

He walked over to the table rubbing his ear. Eric came. Another ghost appeared on the screen. Johnny picked it up and it went out the front door. The girls were watching outside from their cabin. The two walked over to them. Between the moans, chains, and ghost detector, it was loud. The boys and girls pointed the phone towards the forest and followed the sounds, but it was so creepy and real sounding that they ran all the way back to the cabins and locked the door. The four girls with them. The girls felt better in groups of more people. The door was double locked and the curtains shut.

Tina and Terry watched from a window and laughed. That was all the scare they needed. They planned to get the speakers later when there was no way the campers would see them. The speakers were black and could not be seen at night.

The following night the counselors sat drinking punch and playing cards. They could see the campers through the window and they were staying in the same cabin together. "Poor little guys. They don't know their scare is over," Brianna said, but just as she said that the speakers began going off ! And the sounds were by their cabin, and they were not sounds they knew the speakers could make.

"What is that?" Terry asked. "Did you set up those sounds to go off?"

"No," Tina answered. Just then the phone with the app screamed. All three counselors screamed. "I wish I would have spent the summer in college."

The sounds stopped for a minute. "It's those kids. They found the stuff and now they want revenge! They must have been in here," Brianna said. She opened the door up and threw the phone out as it screamed.

Early in the morning Brianna didn't brush her hair and went to the kids cabin and knocked. When Eric answered she said, "Did you guys place those speakers by our cabin? They were moaning all night. We didn't sleep well."

"No," Eric said. "We haven't seen them ever." The speakers could be seen near by in a clear dirt area. The girls stepped up behind him.

"Who said you could be with the girls? You can't stay with them," Brianna screeched.

"They came to stay with us because they were scared," Eric said as the girls nodded.

Brianna couldn't deny them that. She picked up the small speakers and took them to her cabin. That night they began going off. Brianna picked them up and threw them outside. They screamed in protest as if someone was inside. She locked the door and went to bed.

In the morning when she woke and looked out the window she saw it had rained. There were puddles and the campers weren't doing anything outside. She went out and took the speakers. Water poured out of them. They were ruined by the summer rain. "There's nothing like a good summer rain."

Later after breakfast Tina shared with the other two that she saw a ghost when she was watching the rain out the window. It flew out of the speakers and stared into a window for five minutes, and then vanished. "These woods are really haunted," she said.

"Looks like the kids were proven innocent. What will we do for them?" Terry asked Brianna.

"It's going to be rainy. We'll give them free time. I wish they weren't sharing a cabin with girls. Johnny and Patty are holding hands and taking a walk. They are going to be cold," Brianna said with a giggle.

The Ghostly Counselors

A
fter they walked away from the new camper circle they followed the counselors to their new rooms to put their suitcases down. Heading there, the campers passed a cabin that looked abandoned. It was dusty and the roof was coming apart. The campers stopped and stared at the front red door. "That is the forbidden bunk," Brianna told them.

"What happened here?" a new camper asked. They could see through the window there was nothing but bunks, a trunk, and broken wood.

"It's haunted," Eric said. "A kid died there."

"How?" the camper asked.

"Snake bite. It got into his bed. Now if you get bit by a snake you go straight to the nurses," Tony said.

"Is that true?" the new camper Brian asked.

"Yes, and it's haunted," Eric answered. Brian gave him the side eye not wanting to believe it.

"We'll sneak in and go tonight. If his ghost is out we will then prove someone died there. He's not the only camper who's died here, and kids have died at other camps too," Eric explained. "We will go with Tony and Melissa tomorrow night through the window. Are you in?" he asked.

"Yes, sounds pretty creepy," Brian answered.

"You guys come on now!" Brianna was standing by the newbies cabin with the doors wide open. Her hair was a mess from the heat and she wanted them to get in and settled.

They went inside the cabin and she said, "Lunch is at twelve and dinner at six. You can have snacks in between. Everything is at the food hall. You saw it when you were coming this way. You're not supposed to bring snack inside your cabin because of ants," Brianna explained. "We have new activities for you guys every week, and some campers do work. We also have rainy days when you can do whatever you want inside. Some kids like to hang out in the food hall. It's big. There are some other places we don't use any more like the boathouse. We found they were dangerous." She failed to tell them kids died there because they probably wouldn't believe it. Some kids drowned inside the boathouse and some fell out of boats in raging water. "The funnest time is sitting around a fire snacking and telling stories. Welcome to Camp Woodchuck," she said and walked away grinning out the door.

The following night came quickly as they got ready to go and see the forbidden cabin. It was just before midnight and Brian asked, "Do you guys sneak in a lot?"

"No, just a couple times. We had to see it and then once on Halloween. Are you ready to go?" Eric asked.

"Yes," Brian responded and they two boys left quietly with Melissa. The cabin wasn't far. It was the last one. A lonely run down unused shell. They walked there behind trees Eric went to the back window to open it. The moon was full and the wind howled. He pulled it up.

Eric crawled into the window sill and dropped to the other side. The dust made him sneeze.

"Are you okay?" Brian asked.

"Yeah, come on," Eric said and turned on his flashlight.

Eric entered the window. "What is all thi stuff?"

"Broken junk," Eric answered.

Brian opened the trunk. Inside there was a fishing knife and dirty old compass. "This will come in handy when we go on a long hike." He put them in his pocket. A cold breeze blew, but they were warm because of their hoodies. When Brian turned around he thought he saw someone. "Right there. I swear I saw a dark haired boy in the corner of my eye!"

"Yeah?" Eric's eyes were wide.

"Where's the actual bunk?" Brian asked.

"Follow me." Eric directed him to a dark corner in the bunk house. Someone came up behind them and the boys yelled. It was Melissa. She laughed.

"Gosh, You scared the heck out of us!" Eric complained. "Where were you?"

"I was looking around," Melissa explained.

They brought their attention back to where it was. A very rundown bunk they weren't supposed to be looking at. It was very dusty and the blanket was torn. Suddenly, the window they came through slammed. The trio walked to the door, and the doorknob turned like someone was trying to get in and couldn't.

They ran back to their window they came in and heard a voice say, "Give me back my stuff and get out!" It was the boy ghost.

As fast as they could they opened a different window and jumped out running all the way back to their cabins. A few times they heard small footsteps outside, but didn't look.

Come morning they didn't say much about what happened, and knew it had been proven. They went on with activities as usual. What had happened was only between the three of them.

But it didn't take long for the former days activity to catch up with them. As they were walking back from Melissa's cabin they heard talking and shouting coming from the old boathouse. It had gotten dark and they tried to see the way by moonlight. When they got there, the doors were shut and they didn't see anybody, but then a pale white boy floated to the back of the boathouse. They ran to it and looked in the back. No one was there.

Eric and Brian went around to the front of the boathouse and opened the door. The wind was rocking the water because a summer rain was coming. When Brian grabbed the door they heard it. A boy's voice calling help me. They ran back to the cabin as fast as they could. "I think someone died there," Eric said to Brian, and he nodded in agreement because the kid's ghost they saw was going to the boathouse like he belonged there.

They both hoped they wouldn't see any more ghosts the following night. They tried to stay up and they played cards. Johnny was with them. "Hey guys. Where did you get this?" He said holding the knife Brian found at the forbidden cabin.

"I found that, near the forbidden cabin. It was probably a fishing knife," Brian said. As soon as he said that they heard counselors saying things loudly outside and when they looked out the drapes they saw not three but five counselors, and they had no feet! They were specters floating around talking to each other. When one of them knocked on a cabin door the boys hid from the window.

The ghostly voice said, "Do you have the knife and compass that was taken?"

That's when the boys knew they needed to put it back. "We'll go back in the morning and put back the things that I took," Brian said.

The other boys nodded. "It looks like that's what they want. When we give it back, maybe they'll stop haunting," Eric said.

"I'm not staying in a haunted camp," Johnny said. "We could run away and take a bus."

"You're right. I don't want to be here," Brian said.

"We still have to take the stuff back," Eric said. "Then probably stay. Doesn't this place seem desolate?"

"Yeah," the other boys agreed.

"It's late," Johnny said.

"First thing in the morning we'll take the stuff they want back. That should stop the hauntings," Eric said.

The counselors continued through the night knocking on doors. They flew from cabin to cabin knocking on doors and asking, "Do you have the fishing knife and compass from the abandoned cabin?" Some kids called out no.

Eric took the knife and compass and put them under a suitcase in the closet. When the ghost came to their door and asked if they had them they said no. They held their breathes and the ghost didn't respond. When they looked out the window, they could see the ghosts looking all around.

They woke to the sound of birds. When they opened the door they just saw boys and girls talking. Finally Melissa came. "Did you hear that last night? There were ghosts of counselors everywhere!" she squealed. "Maybe they'll close down." She smiled.

"They wanted the stuff we took from the cabin. We're going back now. Want to come?" Eric asked.

"Yes," Melissa answered and they headed down to the old ramshackle cabin.

Brian took the camping items out of his pocket and when Eric opened the window, he threw them through it. "Thanks," came back from the boys ghost. All three ran and the window fell shut.

That day activities went on as usual. Eric, Brian, and Johnny all went fishing by the abandoned boathouse. They did not see any ghosts, but they still decided to move to a place with more clearer water. They suspected someone had died there and they were right.

When they asked Briana about it she said, "More than one kid has died there. We won't be using it any more. We are taking out the boats. They will be near the dock."

Summer Job Night Watch

A

s Herb passed out tickets for people to ride the roller coaster, he recognized a familiar head of blond hair.

"Two tickets please," his ex Trista said.

Herb pushed his glasses up and glanced over at the sunset. He passed her two tickets as she smiled widely at him, poured out her drink, and took a seat. No body was told, they just got on and the bar went down to keep them secure. Herb went to start the ride. He had found this job at the fair with his friends Keith, Nina, and Gale. It was only a summer job working nights and in the fall they would go back to college, but it was an area with crime by the water that desperately needed someone to work nights and it was perfect. The pay wasn't bad either.

He hit start on the ride and it began going fast. He could see where the moon was coming out and liked to watch people scream and laugh on the ride. The sunset was beautiful. The shades of yellow, pink, and blue were fading away as dark took over. He glanced over at his friend Keith and suddenly as Trista went by screaming, a newspaper page blew over by him. It looked like it came from the coaster. He picked it up and read it. It said, **Serial Killer Still on the Loose Near Cold River.** A shudder ran up and down Herbs spine. A hot wind blew. The frightened screams of the people on his ride starting sounding like victims to him.

The roller coaster came to a stop and he watched the people get out. He wanted to tell his friends, but ran to the back to get some soda and calm down. Gale was working at the hot dog and popcorn stand that day with Nina.

Walking further down the river he saw splashes of water on the concrete where people played pop the water balloons. It was a way of keeping cool and winning a prize. They won stuffed animals, small ones, and free popcorn and soda. You just needed to be a good shot.

As he stepped in the water, he noticed by a little light something was in it. It was also on his white sneaker. He recognized it as blood in the water. At first he thought maybe someone cut themselves with a dart, but there was a lot. It was against his better judgement, but he followed it around the corner to an alley way, water and blood. Strangely it just stopped, so he walked to the river but could barely see in it. It got very dark. He looked to his right, but no one was at the water balloon game any more. When he turned around he saw a streetlight flicker on and when it did there was a man standing there with a large knife. It looked like it was dripping. *The blood.*

Herb started running to where there were people screaming, "Keith! Keith!" Keith stopped and stared. "Let's find the girls and get out of here. There's a killer." Both guys ran to get Nina and Gale. There were other people to run concession stands.

They began running to their cars and when Herb turned around and saw the killer in the large jacket following them, he did not see Gale. "Where's Gale? Were did she go?"

"I don't know," his friends answered.

"I'm going back," Herb said. Maybe she took a detour and parked by the water, or saw him coming and hid in a stand. The killer was getting closer so Keith and Nina ran for their cars with the killer behind. That gave Herb some time to find Gale. He started looking through lines and behind stands, but didn't find her. He didn't want to lose her. She had long shiny raven hair and crystal water blue eyes. They were just friends, but could be more in the future.

Herb looked everywhere for her. There wasn't as many people at night, and definitely not as many kids. He ran back to the river and when he looked over at the ferris wheel there she was at the bottom waiting to get away there. When he heard Keith yell while trying to get into his car, he ran to the Ferris wheel and sat next to Gale. It started and they went to the top. It stayed there and people started yelling, but it didn't start. The person running it saw the killer coming and ran away.

The killer began pushing all the buttons trying to get them down but none of them worked. The buttons lit up and then sparked causing people to gasp as the lights went out. He couldn't kill everyone on the ride so he wanted the two he was chasing. A lot of people at the bottom got off and people closer to the ground jumped off but Gale and Herb were stuck at the very top. "Help, help," Herb yelled while everyone ran. Gale began whimpering and as they looked down they saw the killer climbing the ride. As he got closer, Herb and Gale started sliding down. They needed to get out now. Herb was the first one to make it to the bottom. He ran to the controls and turned it on knowing the killer clung for life at the top of it hanging on to the car.

He hung there for a while, but when it became a struggle, Herb stopped the wheel two hundred feet in the air and the killer fell from the jerk of the ride. He hit the cement so hard they heard a crack and did not move because he was dead. As the two walked to the parking lot Herb said, "I'll give you a ride," and when she agreed they turned and saw Keith. He was lying in a pool of blood. The killer had gotten him.

The two called the police from the fair and it didn't take them long to find a body in the river. It was the man who ran the water balloon stand. "The fella must have lost," the officer said about the murderer.

They had caught the Cold River Killer and Herb was a hero. He was in the newspaper the next day. He had luckily also landed his first date with Gale promising himself to protect her forever. They talked to Nina and she was shaken, but had made it home in one piece. They went down in town history as the trio to serve justice on a madman who fed on innocent people. That area did become haunted and when fall came people went to see it and look for ghosts, the most famous one being the man who worked by the river with water balloons. People said they could see him around midnight, and sometimes after come out of the water and look for people to scare. Water was an element the ghost liked. And sometimes people saw the killer watching them with his knife before he vanished, but psychics just said it was a residual haunting and possibly his strong negative energy left behind. Either way, it's lore of Cold River.

Mimicry in the June Moonlight

M

y stepfather-in-law, Arthur, is in jail for attempting to poison me. Now I understand he thought he was being merciful one year ago. My stepfather-in-law tried to murder me. He orchestrated it meticulously: the drive up to the cottage by the lake that his family owned, lacing my tea with oleander extract, leaving a note nearby suggesting my despair had become too much. His twisted version of kindness, I suppose. Either way, he likely would have gotten away with it.

He hadn't anticipated the early rainfall, though, hadn't considered that a park ranger would be doing a routine check and find my car, then me, barely conscious from the toxin, clutching the note, seriously considering its implication after nearly 12 hours of increasing paralysis. There hadn't been a significant storm for weeks. When I woke up in the hospital, my wife, Clara, was by my side, holding my hand, her beautiful face streaked with tears.

Despite my own nausea and weakness, all I wanted was to soothe her distress, so I gently squeezed her hand with what little strength I had. "I... I was so worried. What happened?" she pleaded, hazel eyes brimming with tears. The doctor came in and checked my pulse, then told my wife that I needed to rest. I was grateful for the interruption because I knew once I revealed the truth, my wife's heart would shatter irrevocably. Her stepfather had always been a pillar in her life. I met Clara at university 5 years ago. She was studying literature, and I was in the computer science department. We were both in our early twenties, and I knew within twenty minutes of our first conversation that I wanted to build a life with her. She was intelligent, witty, perceptive, and it didn't hurt that she had striking hazel eyes and dark curly hair. Six months into our relationship, she introduced me to her family. I come from a small family, just my parents and my younger sister.

Our holiday dinners are cozy, intimate gatherings at our house with maybe five people present. But Clara was immediately comfortable with my family, and they adored her. She fit right in, like a perfectly placed comma in a sentence. Everything was progressing beautifully until Clara felt it was time for me to meet her only remaining family member, her stepfather. Arthur Finch was a lean, weathered man who favored flannel shirts and looked like a retired fisherman. He lived in a small house on the outskirts of town, near the river docks. When he gave me a curt nod, his gray eyes seemed distant, and a slight unease settled over me. After we stepped into the one-story house behind him, the first subtle sign should have been the absence of any photos of Clara's mother. Not a single one. In fact, if I truly reflected on it, Clara rarely spoke about her mother. I should have inquired more, but I suppose I always just assumed it was a sensitive topic for her.

The first time a flicker of suspicion crossed my mind about her stepfather was during that visit. I distinctly heard Clara remind her stepfather over the phone multiple times that I had a severe shellfish allergy. Yet, when we sat down for dinner, he served a seafood stew. Fortunately, Clara noticed my hesitation before I took a bite, but if she hadn't, the consequences could have been dire. Then, it was shortly after our engagement when he knew I was a novice sailor, but I'm fairly certain he loosened a railing on his sailboat when the three of us were out on the water. The third instance, however, was undeniable. If that hiker hadn't stumbled upon my barely conscious form by the roadside, I'm sure I would have succumbed to the poison. You might be wondering why I continued to interact with a man I suspected of trying to harm me, but my mind kept rationalizing those earlier events as misunderstandings or coincidences. Also, Clara was eager for her stepfather and me to have a better relationship, and I couldn't bear to distress her. I'll never forget the drive to the cottage.

My stepfather-in-law was a man of few words, so when he decided to share an anecdote, I almost felt a sense of relief that I didn't have to keep the conversation going. He kept his gaze fixed on the road and said, "There once was a young woman who lived a peaceful life with her family in the valley. It was her, two sisters, her parents, her grandmother, her uncles and aunts, and all her cousins. She didn't know much about the world beyond her family's farm, but she had countless chores to do, so she never yearned to leave. For a time, all was harmonious, as it should be. The young woman and her family lived off the land, farmed, and prospered until one day, on her 21st birthday, the young woman saw the figure in black at the edge of the fields, gaunt and still. It seemed to absorb the light around it. When she asked her father about it, he warned her to stay away from the figure, that nothing good ever came from the outer edges of the valley on a moonless night." We were nearing the cottage now, and as we approached it, a strange feeling began to creep up my spine, a sense of foreboding gripping me tightly. "The young woman heeded her father for three days. On the fourth night, she found herself outside the house, walking towards the fields. As she drew closer, she saw the figure's face: hollow eyes, a thin, cruel mouth, and skin that seemed stretched too tightly over bone. Its mortal mind couldn't comprehend the emptiness it radiated.

The figure offered her a withered hand. Mesmerized, she reached out and took it." He parked the car and turned off the engine, but still wouldn't look at me. Instead, he stared ahead into the dense trees surrounding the lake and finished his unsettling tale. "The moment she took that hand, the shadow claimed her. They found her six months later at the bottom of a ravine, living in a makeshift shelter, emaciated and delirious, speaking in rhymes and nonsense. What was disturbing was that both her hands, from the wrists downward, were gone, and yet the wounds were crudely bandaged, and someone or something had clearly been providing her with sustenance. Her parents brought her home and tried to nurse her back to health. The healers fitted her with artificial hands, which she constantly tried to remove, but the young woman was never truly the same again. When she began to slowly speak coherently again, she spoke of a being with eyes like pools of tar, a long, skeletal body covered in shadows, thorns instead of fingernails, clumps of black hair that seemed to writhe on their own, and then finally, a chilling whisper." He fell silent, and a shiver ran down my spine. I asked him what happened to her.

My stepfather-in-law snapped out of his reverie and looked at me, his expression unreadable. "Let me show you the best fishing spots." The trial was swift. My stepfather-in-law was found in possession of a vial containing traces of oleander and several online articles detailing its effects. His internet search history revealed numerous queries about lethal plant toxins. When Arthur Finch was incarcerated, my wife cried herself to sleep every night for weeks. I think she harbored resentment towards me for what happened, even though she never voiced those feelings. I would often catch her gazing out the window of our apartment in the direction of the lake, which we could vaguely see in the distance. She became increasingly withdrawn, took a leave of absence from her job, and would sleep for most of the day. Some days, she wouldn't even get out of bed. Her face grew gaunt, and sometimes when I saw her frail form in the dim light of our bedroom, I could almost see the outline of her bones beneath her skin. Her sadness threatened to consume her, and I felt helpless to stop it.

One afternoon, I returned home, and she wasn't there. I searched for her everywhere in the apartment. I don't know how I knew, but somehow I felt she would be at the cottage. I jumped into my car and drove there as fast as I dared, not caring about potential speeding tickets. I arrived just as dusk was settling, and I saw her. She was standing at the edge of the lake, her back to me, facing the dark water. "Clara?" I called her name as I got out of the car. She didn't turn to acknowledge me; instead, she remained motionless, her tangled dark hair swaying slightly in the gentle breeze. I called to her again, a deep sense of dread settling in my stomach. Slowly, Clara turned to face me, and that's when I saw her face: gaunt, the skin stretched taut, her eyes wide and black, reflecting no light. That's when she let out a chilling whisper, a sound that seemed to vibrate in the very air around me. A sharp pain shot through my head, and I instinctively clapped my hands over my ears. I tried calling my wife's name again, but all I could hear was the whisper, which was starting to feel like icy fingers tracing patterns on my brain. My vision blurred, and I stumbled backward. A dozen figures had emerged from the trees, all of them with gaunt faces, wide black eyes, and the same unsettling stillness that had replaced my wife's bright hazel ones, and they were all moving towards me. Without even thinking, I scrambled back into my car, started the engine, my ears ringing from the sound of the whisper. I drove away.

Three days later, I'm staying on a friend's sofa. After the doctors had examined me, they said it was a miracle I hadn't suffered permanent hearing loss from the intensity of the sound. I just nodded and let them continue their assessment. A persistent ringing filled my ears, a sound I couldn't seem to shake. There was no way I could explain what I had witnessed by the lake to them. I'm waiting for the ringing and the lingering headache to subside before I go looking for Clara again. This time, I will be prepared. I've already spoken to the local authorities, but I know their search efforts won't have the same urgency as mine. My phone buzzes, and I cautiously hold it to my less affected ear. It's a restricted call from the detention center. I accept it because who else could possibly offer any answers? "It happened, didn't it?" my stepfather-in-law's raspy voice made me flinch. I swallowed hard. "Clara's gone," I said numbly. "She's returned to where she belongs," he replied. "How am I lucky?" I asked, a bitter anger rising within me. "She was my wife, and your stepdaughter." "That thing was neither a daughter nor a wife. It knows how to mimic humanity. Why do you think I told you that story?" His voice was low and menacing, and my jaw dropped.

Was he seriously suggesting he was the young woman from his dark tale? "You're cruel, disowning your stepdaughter, trying to poison me."

"You need to listen to me, boy, and listen carefully.

That creature was left on my doorstep a few months after I returned from the river. It was an infant then, and it destroyed my wife. I found pieces of her around their bedroom for years. Then, it proceeded to isolate me, ensuring no one close to me survived. It wouldn't let me die or end its own existence, and I couldn't understand why until I realized it needed me the way a predator needs its territory. Finally, when everyone I cared about was gone, it needed new prey, and it found you. It will take pieces of you, then keep you alive to take pieces of everyone you will ever love. It will feed on your despair as you endure your own personal hell." I swallowed hard. He had clearly lost his grip on reality. What on earth was he trying to convey? "If I were you, I would gather your belongings and leave. Leave this town, hell, leave this state. Don't ever look back, you hear me? Ever." With a sharp click, he hung up. I wish I had heeded his words. I wish I hadn't been so determined to rescue my wife at any cost. Instead, I am sitting here in the dim light inside the old cottage, peering out the window. My fingers are wrapped tightly around a fishing knife. A sliver of moon casts an eerie glow, the only illumination in the pitch-black night, and there, in the darkness, I think I see a figure emerge from the trees. She almost resembles my wife... almost, until her face contorts, her eyes become vacant pools, and she whispers.

The Closet's Secret

D

uring the summer of 2023, my 6-year-old, Leo, and I played a lot of hide-and-seek. Well, hide-and-seek with a few extra rules: one, I'm the only one who hides; he doesn't want to. Two, I have to call out "Here I am!" every few minutes; otherwise, he'd never find me. Three, when he gets close, I pop a hand or foot out of my hiding spot, and he giggles, "Found you!" Six-year-olds are really funny, okay? And I didn't exactly have the money to buy him a ton of toys.

We just moved out into this apartment a few months ago; the deposit took up nearly my entire paycheck. I got all the kitchenware from a neighbor. We ate pasta and sauce often, and I was still relying on a 15-year-old bicycle. "Hide again," Leo said, pulling my shirt.

"Hide again, but it's almost supper time, please?"

"Okay, but only two more rounds. Okay, go count in the living room." He scurried around the corner as fast as he could. "1, 2, 3..." I dashed through the hallway, and then I saw it: the linen closet. Perfect. I slid the door open and squeezed inside. It was a tight squeeze, all those scratchy, wool blankets pressing against me, but it was worth it because the better the hiding spot, the more time I got to myself. I pulled out my e-reader and started browsing a novel. Soon, his light footsteps echoed from the kitchen. I waited a moment; when he didn't seem to be coming my way, I nudged the door. "Here I am!" I called out.

Footsteps grew closer. I heard his soft chuckles as he walked towards me, and then he started going down the stairs. What a silly goose. I pushed the door open a little further, just in time to see his little sneakers disappear from the bottom step. Then I smiled. More quiet time for me. I leaned back against the shelf in the closet and pulled out the e-reader. "Mama," I heard him whisper from downstairs. "Mama, where are you?" I chuckled. I wonder if a parent invented hide-and-seek. It's quite ingenious; you get a few precious minutes of peace. They're not even supposed to make much noise. You're keeping them occupied at the same time.

Absolutely. "Here I am!" I tensed; every muscle in my body tightened. But I heard it clear as day, a low, clear voice calling from downstairs. But Leo and I were home alone. Oh no, someone's in the apartment. "And Leo!" I scrambled out of the closet. "Leo, where are you?" I heard Leo's footsteps running below me, his chuckles floating up to me. I couldn't move, couldn't breathe. "Leo!" I finally yelled. More chuckles, and then Leo's voice, "I see your shoes!" No. I bolted down the steps, shouting for him. I rushed into the dining room, and he wasn't there, just his empty race car rug, toy trucks scattered, bright colors staring back at me. I ran back into the hallway, spinning around. "Leo?" But I didn't hear any footsteps, any chuckling. The apartment was completely silent now, and I could hear my own breathing. I ran into the spare bedroom. It was empty. I ran over to the wardrobe, yanked it open, looked high and low. Nothing. Stumbling back out into the hallway, I crossed back towards our bedroom, the only bedroom left. I ran inside and flipped on the lamp. Empty. The pile of clean laundry on the dresser untouched, the closet door ajar, my sweaters inside, the cushions tossed onto the floor in a jumble. Heart pounding, I ran around the other side of the bed. Also empty. I bent down to look under the bed. Empty. "Mama?" Relief washed over me as I heard that voice. The door to the washroom creaked open, and one brown eye peeked out at me, wide with fright. I ran over and scooped him up, hugged him tightly, and then I lifted him up and headed for the washroom. His eyes were still wide with fright, and they weren't focused on my face but the spot just above my shoulder.

I spun around. It took me a moment to see it, but then I did. I stared at the wardrobe, rooted to the spot, my heart hammering in my chest. In the shadows, peeking out from underneath the edges of my blouses and jackets, were two bare feet. In moments like this, my brain doesn't really process; it's too slow. Pure instinct takes over. The logical thing would have been to lock ourselves in the washroom and call for help, but instead, I just sprinted for the front door as fast as I could. As I ran out into the hallway, I heard the heavy footsteps, slow and deliberate, echoing through the apartment. I could still hear them pounding in my ears as I ran to the superintendent and cried for help. The police arrived; they searched the apartment. They didn't find anything, no signs of forced entry either. So they assured me they'd keep an eye on our building for the next few days, but that was all they could really do.

I decided to stay at my sister's place for a few weeks until I felt safe again, but every time I closed my eyes, I could see them, those two feet that looked so unnatural somehow, elongated as if stretched, a bit too pale in color to belong to any normal person, toenails yellowed and thick. And I think back to that wardrobe, how I'd gotten it for free from an online forum, how the poster mentioned their grandfather had passed away, and they were just trying to clear out his belongings quickly. And I wondered, what was the cause of death?

The Vanished Friend

T

his story has been a mystery in our family for three generations. I often visited my great-aunt Clara as a young girl. My great-aunt was a petite, energetic woman with a laugh that could fill a room. We bonded despite the age difference, and I always looked forward to our visits. But one afternoon, something shifted. It was just the two of us in her sunroom; my grandparents had gone shopping, leaving me with her. I remember walking in to find her sitting in her wicker chair, but she was different. She was unusually still, her expression pensive, and the familiar sparkle in her eyes was gone, replaced by a profound, unsettling seriousness. I could sense a shift in the atmosphere, and despite my usual playful nature, I felt the weight of her quietness.

At first, I wasn't sure how to approach her. I was just a child, but even then, I could feel the strangeness in the air. Finally, I blurted out, "What's wrong, Nana Clara?" I always called her that, and it usually made her smile, but today it felt like a weak attempt to break the heavy silence. Her brow furrowed, and a faint, sad smile touched her lips. "Would you think I was imagining things if I told you something odd?" she asked. It was so unlike her that I instinctively took a step back. I hadn't expected such a serious tone. "What is it about?" I asked hesitantly. "A strange memory... a friend who vanished." I was a little bit confused. "Okay," I said softly, and then she began her story. "I grew up with a boy named Alistair. He lived on the next farm over. We were inseparable from kindergarten all the way through college.

After graduation, I moved to the city for work, and he went overseas to teach. We exchanged letters for a while, but life got busy, and we lost touch for about eight years. When I finally moved back to the countryside, I looked him up, and we decided to go hiking one weekend, something we used to do all the time." She paused, the memory clearly taking her to a difficult place. Her hands tightened on the armrests of the chair, and I could feel her distress intensifying. "That morning, there was a feeling in the air, a subtle wrongness. Just a knot of unease in my stomach. I almost canceled, but I dismissed it as pre-hike jitters. Alistair mentioned feeling a bit off, too, with a headache on the drive to the trail, but we brushed it aside. The trail was overgrown, not how I remembered it. When we reached a familiar overlook, something was different. There was a rock formation I didn't recognize, and the light seemed too sharp, almost artificial. My instincts were screaming at me to turn back, but I kept going. I walked a little further, and that's when I heard it: a humming sound, a faint vibration. It was close, almost beside me.

The breeze picked up, swirling around us as if it had its own energy, and that's when I turned to point something out to Alistair, but he wasn't there. I called his name. Nothing. I shouted, but there was no reply. My heart started to race, and a wave of panic washed over me. I turned and hurried back to where we started, but when I got there, his car was gone. I could feel my breath catching in my throat as she spoke. I could almost picture it: the isolation, the growing terror. "I drove back frantic, convinced he'd played some kind of cruel joke. I went straight to his family's farm, but when I got there, his parents were in the kitchen. I asked them when Alistair would be home, but they looked at me with bewildered expressions. They told me they didn't have a son named Alistair. He was never part of their family. I was utterly lost. I started asking around the small town.

No one knew him. No one had ever heard of him. He wasn't in any of my old school photos. I couldn't find his name on any lists." She let out a small, shaky laugh, but it held no amusement. "The only thing I had was a map we'd used for the hike. It's faded now, but his initials are still marked on our intended route, where we planned to stop for lunch. But no one, not a single soul, could remember him. Alistair was gone, as if he'd never existed at all." There was a long silence then, and I could feel the weight of her unspoken thoughts hanging in the air. Her gaze was distant, and the sadness in her eyes was profound. I wanted to say something comforting, but I was speechless, caught in the same haunted silence as she was, not knowing what to do. Finally, I reached out and took her hand. She seemed lost in her own world, and I began to worry that she was becoming confused.

When my grandmother came to pick me up, I mentioned to her that I thought Nana Clara might need more company, that she seemed a little lost in her memories. But then my grandmother stopped me before I could say more. "She's not confused about that," my grandmother said, her voice quiet but with an odd, almost fearful undertone. "She's been telling that story since your mother was a little girl. I believe her, or at least I believe she believes it." Those words unsettled me deeply. My grandmother was a practical woman, not one for fanciful tales, so for her to say that sent a shiver down my spine. I've never forgotten that story or the marked map. It's still tucked away in a box, worn and creased, but the initials 'A.M.' remain, a reminder of something I can't explain. And as the years pass, I often wonder what truly happened that strange day, so long ago. Did Alistair somehow step outside of our reality and get pulled into another time, another dimension, perhaps, where his life was never ours? But I trust my great-aunt's memory. Maybe one day, someone will understand it better than I do.

A Glitch in the Night

W

hen I was 16, we went to my friend Liam's house for a gathering. His house was on the edge of our small village in rural Scotland, miles away from anyone else. It was the kind of isolated place where you could almost hear the stillness of the land – no traffic, no noise, just fields stretching out. It was the early 2000s, and we were all typical 15 to 16-year-olds, living for the usual fizzy drinks, loud music, and laughter, and of course, the company of girls. We were sleeping in his back garden in a couple of tents we'd pitched beside the old stone wall.

The patch of rough ground beyond the garden was our hangout for the night. We'd decided to build a small bonfire with some fallen branches and bits of wood we'd gathered. It took a few tries, but after some effort, we finally got it going. There we were, sitting around the crackling fire, passing around bottles of Irn-Bru, laughing, joking, and acting like typical teenagers. Then, Ewan, the one whose house it was, suggested we go to the old standing stones. His tone was casual but also held a hint of something more, an idea we couldn't ignore. We all agreed to go, not giving it much thought at the time. It was only a five-minute walk across the field, he said. Now, here's the thing about standing stones in Scottish folklore. These aren't just random rocks; they're ancient monuments, often arranged in circles, remnants of a distant past.

But what makes them even more intriguing is the belief that they are places imbued with a certain energy, perhaps even connected to other realms. So, we left the small fire, though not before a couple of my friends playfully scattered some dirt on it, making sure it was mostly out, laughing and chatting as we made our way across the dewy field. The night was cool, the stars were bright, and everything felt pretty normal until we reached the standing stones. The place felt different from the moment we stepped within the circle. It's hard to articulate, but imagine walking into a small grove of ancient trees, stepping onto ground that feels strangely firm, where the air suddenly feels crisper. Even though it was late spring, it felt like we had walked into a pocket of early autumn. The temperature seemed to drop a few degrees instantly, and the atmosphere felt still, almost expectant. I remember the quiet, the kind that feels profound. We stood there for a few moments, messing around, trying to shrug off the odd feeling, but one by one, my friends started to sense it too – the feeling that we shouldn't linger. It was almost as if the stones themselves were radiating a subtle warning.

Ewan, the one who had suggested the standing stones in the first place, was the first to say, "Right, this is a bit weird. Let's head back." And everyone agreed immediately, without question. The walk back felt quicker, like something was nudging us along. And as we approached the area where the bonfire had been, one of my friends exclaimed, "Look! It's still burning!" We all stopped dead in our tracks, staring at the faint glow in the distance. It was impossible; we'd mostly put it out. Yet, there it was, a small but definite flame flickering. There were no other houses nearby, so no one could have come by and relit it. The fire was in the exact same spot as when we left it, a tiny orange glow against the dark. That's when the unease settled in. We started walking towards it again, a little faster now, hearts beating a bit quicker with each step. We were drawn to something we couldn't understand. And then, as we got closer, there it was, exactly as it had been before – a small patch of glowing embers, barely alight.

The ashes hadn't been disturbed. It was as if a few minutes had simply been skipped. A heavy silence followed. None of us could speak. The realization hit us all at once, a shared understanding that defied logic and reason. We stared at the dying embers for what felt like a long time, and in that moment, it was like the world around us had held its breath. We hurried back to the tents, not saying a word to each other. There was no need; we were all thinking the same thing. It was as though we'd brushed against something ancient and unknown. When we got to the tents, we tried to rationalize it – maybe a badger had stirred the embers, causing them to reignite slightly while we were gone.

But we'd only been gone for about fifteen minutes; the embers should have been completely cold by then, not glowing. One of my friends was so spooked by what we had witnessed that he called his older sister to come and get him. He left, clearly shaken. We never really spoke of it again. It's one of those things that's impossible to properly explain, something that unless you've experienced it, you would never truly believe. But I'll never forget it. I can still see that faint glow in the darkness, a tiny defiance of the natural order, as if we had glimpsed something just beyond our comprehension.

Page |